BRIAR
ROSE

Works By Robert Coover

Short Fiction

PRICKSONGS AND DESCANTS

IN BED ONE NIGHT & OTHER BRIEF ENCOUNTERS

A NIGHT AT THE MOVIES

Plays

A THEOLOGICAL POSITION

Novels

GERALD'S PARTY

THE ORIGIN OF THE BRUNISTS

THE UNIVERSAL BASEBALL ASSOCIATION, INC.
J. HENRY WAUGH, PROP.

A POLITICAL FABLE

SPANKING THE MAID

WHATEVER HAPPENED TO GLOOMY GUS OF THE CHICAGO BEARS?

PINOCCHIO IN VENICE

JOHN'S WIFE

BRIAR ROSE

THE PUBLIC BURNING

GHOST TOWN

THE ADVENTURES OF LUCKY PIERRE

BRIAR ROSE

ROBERT COOVER

GROVE PRESS

New York

A different version of this text appeared in *Conjunction 26.*

Published simultaneously in Canada
Printed in the United States of America

Library of Congress Cataloging-in-Publication Data
Coover, Robert.
    Briar Rose / Robert Coover.
        p. cm.
    ISBN-10: 0-8021-3541-2
    ISBN-13: 978-0-8021-3541-4
    1. Sleeping Beauty—Adaptations. 2. Fairy tales—Adaptations.
I. Title.
PS3553.0633B75   1996
813'.54—dc20   96-4917

DESIGN BY LAURA HAMMOND HOUGH

Grove Press
an imprint of Grove/Atlantic, Inc.
841 Broadway
New York, NY 10003

Distributed by Publishers Group West

www.groveatlantic.com

06 07 08 09 10 LS-0606 10 9 8 7 6 5 4 3

for Pili
& all her magic tricks

HE IS SURPRISED TO DISCOVER HOW EASY IT IS. THE BRANCHES part like thighs, the silky petals caress his cheeks. His drawn sword is stained, not with blood, but with dew and pollen. Yet another inflated legend. He has undertaken this great adventure, not for the supposed reward—what is another lonely bedridden princess?—but in order to provoke a confrontation with the awful powers of enchantment itself. To tame mystery. To make, at last, his name. He'd have been better off trying for the runes of wisdom or the Golden Fleece. Even another bloody grail. As the briars, pillowy with a sudden extravagance of fresh blooms, their thorns decorously sheathed in the full moonlight, open up to receive him as a doting mother might, he is pricked only by chagrin. Yet he knows what it has cost others who have gone before him, he can smell their bodies caught in the thicket, can glimpse the pallor of their moon-bleached bones, rattling gently when the soft wind blows. That odor of decay is about the extent of his ordeal, and even it is assuaged by the fragrances of fresh tansy and camomile, roses, lilac and hyssop, lavender and savory, which encompass him affectionately—perhaps he has been chosen, perhaps it is his virtue which has caused the hedge to bloom—as he plunges deeper into the thicket, the castle turrets and battlements already visible to him, almost within reach, through its trembling branches.

SHE DREAMS, AS SHE HAS OFTEN DREAMT, OF ABANDONMENT and betrayal, of lost hope, of the self gone astray from the body, the body forsaking the unlikely self. She feels like a once-proud castle whose walls have collapsed, her halls and towers invaded, not by marauding armies, but by humbler creatures, bats, birds, cats, cattle, her departed self an unkempt army marauding elsewhere in a scatter of confused intentions. Her longing for integrity is, in her spellbound innocence, all she knows of rage and lust, but this longing is itself fragmented and wayward, felt not so much as a monstrous gnawing at the core as more like the restless scurry of vermin in the rubble of her remote defenses, long since fallen and benumbed. What, if anything, can make her whole again? And what is "whole"? Her parents, as always in her dreams, have vanished, gone off to death or the continent or perhaps to one of their houses of pleasure, and she is being stabbed again and again by the treacherous spindle, impregnated with a despair from which, for all her fury, she cannot awaken.

THE PALE MOONLIT TURRETS OF THE CASTLE, GLIMPSED through the brambles, rise high into the black night above like the clenched fists of an unforgiving but stonily silent father, upon whose tender terrain below he is darkly trespassing, heralded by a soft icy clatter of tinkling bones. Unlike these others who ornament the briars, he has come opportunely when the hedge is in full bloom, or perhaps (he prefers to think) the hedge has blossomed tonight because it is he who has come, its seductive caresses welcoming him even as the cold castle overhead repels, the one a promise and a lure, showing him the way, the other the test he must undertake to achieve the object of his heroic quest. Which is? Honor. Knowledge. The exercise of his magical powers. Also love of course. If the old tales be true, a sleeping princess awaits him within. He imagines her as not unlike this soft dew-bedampened wall he is plunging through, silky and fragrant and voluptuously receptive. If she is the symbolic object of his quest, her awakening is not without its promise of passing pleasures. She is said, after all, to be the most beautiful creature in the world, both fair and good, musically gifted, delicate, virtuous and graceful and with the gentle disposition of an angel, and, for all her hundred years and more, still a child, innocent and yielding. Achingly desirable. And desiring. Of course, she is also the daughter of a mother embraced by a frog, and there has been talk about ogres in the family, dominion by sorcery, and congress with witches and wizards and other powers too dark to name. If there be any truth in these century-old rumors from benighted times, this adventure could end, not in love's sweet delirium, but in its pain, its infamous cruelty. This prospect, however, does not dissuade him. On the contrary. It incites him.

Briar Rose

THERE IS THIS TO BE SAID FOR THE STABBING PAIN OF THE spindle prick. It anchors her, locates a self when all else in sleep unbinds and scatters it. When a passing prince asks who she is, she replies simply, having no reply other to offer, I am that hurts. This prince—if prince he be, and who can truly say as he/it drifts shapeshifting past, substantial as a fog at sea?—is but one of countless princes who have visited her in her dreams, her hundred years of dreams, unceasing, without so much as day's respite. None remembered of course, no memory of her dreams at all, each forgotten in the very dreaming of them as though to dream them were to erase them. And yet, so often have her dreams revisited fragments and images of dreams dreamt before, a sort of recognizable architecture has grown up around them, such that, though each dream is, must be, intrinsically unique, there is an ambient familiarity about them all that consoles her as memory might, did she know it, and somewhat teaches her whereto to flee when terror engulfs her like a sudden wicked spell. One such refuge is what she sometimes supposes to be a kitchen or a servery, else a strange gallery with hearth and wooden tub, oft as not at ground level with a packed earthen floor and yet with grand views out an oriel's elevated bay. Sometimes there are walls, doors, ceilings, sometimes not. Sometimes she drifts in and out of this room alone, or it appears, in its drafty solitude, around her, but sometimes familiar faces greet her, if none she knows to name, like all else ever changing. Except for one perhaps: a loving old crone, hideously ugly and vaguely threatening, yet dearer to her in her dreams than any other, even courting princes.

WELL, OLD CRONE. UGLY. THANK YOU VERY MUCH. HAS THAT smug sleeper paused to consider how she will look and smell after a hundred years, lying comatose and untended in an unchanged bed? A century of collected menses alone should stagger the lustiest of princes. The curse of the bad fairy, yes. She has reminded the forgetful creature of this in her dreams, has described the stagnant and verminous pallet whereon she idly snoozes and croned her indelible images of human decrepitude, has recounted for her the ancient legends of saints awaking from a hundred years of sleep, glimpsing with dismay the changes the world has suffered, and immediately crumbling into dust. Her little hearthside entertainments. Which are momentarily disturbing perhaps, causing her charge's inner organs to twitch and burble faintly, but nothing sticks in that wastrel's empty head, nothing except her perverse dream of lovestruck princes. Or maybe she knows, instinctively, about the bewitching power of desire, knows that, in the realm of first kisses, and this first kiss firstmost, she *is* beautiful, must be, the fairy herself will see to that, is obliged to, must freshen her flesh and wipe her bum, costume and coiffure her, sweep the room of all morbidity and cushion her for he who will come in lustrous opulence. Alone, the fragrances at her disposal would make a pope swoon and a saint cast off, his britches afore, eternity. No, all these moral lessons with which the fairy ornaments the century's dreaming are mere fancies invented for her own consolation while awaiting that which she herself, in her ingenerate ambivalence, has ordained.

THOUGH PROUD OF THE HEROIC TASK SET HIM (HE WILL, overcoming all obstacles, teach her who she is, and for his discovery she will love and honor him forever without condition) and impatient with all impediment, he nevertheless does feel impeded, and not so much by the heady blossoms' dense embrace as by his own arousal which their velvety caresses have excited. They seem to be instructing him that the prize here without may well exceed the prize within, that in effect his test lies not before him but behind, already passed, or, rather, that the test is not of his strength and valor but of his judgment: to wit, to choose an imagined future good over a real and present one is to play the fabled fool, is it not? Perhaps that tale the countryman told that put him all on fire to engage upon this fine adventure was but a subtle ruse to lure him to the briar hedge and thus into this profounder examination of his maturity and aplomb. All about him, the swaying remains of his anonymous predecessors clink and titter in the moonlight as though to mock the naive arrogance of his quest (who is he to seek to "make his name" or to penetrate the impenetrable?) and to call him back to the brotherhood of ordinary mortals. If it feels good, do it, he seems to hear their bones whisper in wind-chimed echo of that ancient refrain, and for a moment the hostile castle turrets recede and his eyes, petal-stroked, close and something like pure delight spreads outward from his thorn-tickled loins and fills his body—but then, pricked not by briars but by his own sense of vocation, his commitment to love and adventure and honor and duty, and above all his commitment to the marvelous, his passionate desire to transcend the immediate gratifications of the flesh and to insert himself wholly into that world more world than world, bonding with it indissolubly, his name made not by single feat but by forever-aftering, he plunges forward again (those turrets: where have they gone?), wide-eyed and sword raised high.

*   *   *

HER GHOSTLY PRINCES HAVE COME TO HER SEVERALLY WITH bites and squeezes, probing fingers, slaps and tickles, have pricked her with their swords and switched her thighs with briar stems, have licked her throat and ears, sucked her toes, spilled wine on her or holy water, and with their curious lips have kissed her top to bottom, inside and out, but they have not in these false wakings relieved her ever of her spindled pain. Often they are beautiful, at least at first, with golden bodies and manelike hair and powerful hands and lean rippling flanks, yet are sad and tender in their gaze in the manner of martyred saints; but at other times they are doddering and ugly, toothless, malodorous and ravaged by disease, or become so even as they approach her pallet, a hideous transformation that sends her screaming to the servery, if a servery is what it is, and sometimes they become or are more like beast than man, fanged and clawed and merciless as monsters are said to be. Once (or more than once: she has no memory) she has been visited by her own father, couched speculatively between her thighs, dressed in his crown and cloak and handsome boots and chewing his white beard, a puzzled expression on his kind royal face, as, with velvety thrusts, he searches out the spindle. In her waking life there might have been something wrong about this, but here in sleep (she knows she is asleep and dreaming, a century's custom having this much taught her) it hardly seems to matter and in some wise brings her comfort for he rests lightly on her and softens her cracked lips and nipples with his tears or else his moist paternal tongue, whilst he attends her mother, standing at the bedside with cloths and lotions at his service and offering her advice. Over her head, as though she were not present (and she is not), they lament the loss of their only child and worry about the altered kingdom and whether it can ever be put right again. It's that damned spindle, her mother says. Can't you do something about it? Yes, yes, I'm working on it, he gasps as his face turns red and his eyes pop open and his beard falls off.

✻   ✻   ✻

WHO AM I? SHE WANTS TO KNOW. *WHAT* AM I? WHY THIS curse of an endless stupor and its plague of kissing suitors? Do their ceaseless but ineffectual assaults really prefigure a telling one, or is my credulous anticipation (I have no memory!) merely part of the stuporous and stupefying joke? These are the sorts of childish questions the fairy must try to answer throughout the long night of the hundred-year sleep, as the princess, ever freshly distressed, heaves again and again into what she supposes to be the old castle servery or else her nursery or the musicians' gallery in the great hall, or something of each of these, yet none. Patience, child, the fairy admonishes her. I know it hurts. But stop your whinging. I will tell you who you are. Come here, down this concealed passageway, through this door that is not a door. You are such a door, accessible only to the adept, you are such a secret passageway to nowhere but itself. Now, do you see this narrow slot in the wall from which the archers defend the castle? It is called, like you, a murderess. If you peer through it, perhaps you will see the bones of your victims, rattling in the brambles down below. Like you, this slot has long since fallen into disuse, and, see here, a pretty black spider has built her web in it. You are that still creature, waiting silently for your hapless prey. You are this window, webbed in spellbinding death, this unvisited corridor, that hidden spiral staircase to the forbidden tower, the secret room at the top where pain begins. You are all things dangerous and inviolate. You are she who has renounced the natural functions, she who invades the dreams of the innocent, she who harbors wild forces and so defines and provokes the heroic, and yet you are the magical bride, of all good the bell and flower, she through whom all glory is to be won, love known, the root out of which all need germinates. You are she about whom the poets have written: The rose and thorn, the smile and tear:/The burden of all life's song is here. Do you see this old candleholder? asks the fairy, pointing to the sharp iron spike in the petaled center of the wall bracket lamp by the archers' window. She grasps a slender tallow candle the color of bedridden flesh and with a sudden violent gesture impales it on the spike, causing the sleeper to shriek and shrink away and her dormant

13

heart to pound. With a soft cackle, the fairy lights the candle with her breath and says: You are that flame, flickering like a burning fever in the hearts of men, consuming them with desire, bewitching them with your radiant and mysterious allure. What the fairy does not say, because she does not want to terrify her (always a mess to clean up after, linens to change), is: You are Beauty. She says: When others ask, who am I, what am I, *you* are the measure and warrant of their answers. Rest easy, my child. You are Briar Rose. Your prince will come.

HE, THE CHOSEN ONE, AS HE PRESUMES (I AM HE WHO WILL awaken Beauty!), presses valiantly through the thickening briar hedge, hacking without mercy at the petals that so voluptuously caress him, aware now that they were his first test and that he has perhaps lingered too long in their seductive embrace and so may have already failed in his quest, or may even have made a wrong turning and lost his way: those castle turrets, where *are* they—?! The bones of his ill-fated predecessors clatter ominously in the assaulted branches, and the thorns, exposed by his cropping of the blossoms, snag in his flesh and shred what remains of his clothing. But he is not frightened, not very anyway, nor has he lost any of his manly resolve to see this enterprise through, for he knows this is a marvelous and emblematic journey beyond the beyond, requiring his unwavering courage and dedication, but promising a reward beyond the imagination of ordinary mortals. Still, he wishes he could remember more about who or what set him off on this adventure, and how it is he knows that his commitment and courage are so required. It is almost as though his questing—which is probably not even "his" at all, but rather a something out there in the world beyond this brambly arena into which he has been absorbed, in the way that an idea sucks up thought—were inventing him, from scratch as it were (he is not without his lighter virtues): is this what it means "to make one's name"? In reply, all around him, the pendulous bones whisper severally in fugal refrain: I am he who will awaken Beauty! I am he who will awaken Beauty! I am he who will awaken Beauty!

* * *

HER TRUE PRINCE HAS COME AT LAST, JUST AS PROMISED! HE
is lean and strong with flowing locks, just a little hair
around his snout and dirt under his nails, but otherwise a
handsome and majestic youth, worthy of her and of her
magical disenchantment. She sleeps still, eyes closed, and
yet she sees him as he bends toward her, brushing her breast
with one paw—hand, rather—and easing her thighs apart
with the other, his eyes aglow with a transcendental love.
It is happening! It is really happening! she thinks as he lowers his subtle weight upon her as a fur coverlet might be
laid upon a featherbed. The only thing unusual about her
awakening is that it is taking place in the family chapel
and she is stretched out in her silken chemise on the
wooden altar, itself draped for the occasion in fine dam-
ask. Her parents are watching from the upper gallery, having just wandered in from their bedchamber, her father still
pulling on his cream-colored woolen drawers, her mother
dressed in a long black tunic, clasped at the throat with a

ruby brooch. Below them stand the steward and the mar-
shal and the cook and the butler and chamberlain, the
entire staff of domestic servants and household knights,
but they all seem to be dead. No, they are merely asleep,
awaiting your own awakening, explains the old crone,
midwifing her prince's kiss, who seems not to know how
it is done. His mouth approaches hers and she is filled with
his presence, it is as though he is melting into her body or
she into his, but when in joy (the new day dawns at last!)
she opens her eyes he is nowhere to be found, nor is she in
the chapel nor in her sickbed either. She is in what is probably the kitchen, where the familiar old crone, her head
wreathed in a flickering glitter of tiny blue lights like
otherworldly fireflies, is sitting by a door that is not a door,
one leading to a hidden corridor (she does not know how
she knows this to be true), slitting the white throat of a
trussed piglet, which is squealing madly as though for a
mother who has abandoned him. Probably this has happened before, perhaps many times, she doesn't remember,
can't remember. Who am I? she demands. *What* am I? The
crone hangs the gurgling piglet by its trotters on a beam
to let it drain and says: Calm down, child. Let me tell you
a story . . .

THERE WAS ONCE A BEAUTIFUL YOUNG PRINCESS, RELATES THE
fairy, who, for reasons of mischief, her own or someone else's,
got something stuck under her fingernail, a thorn perhaps,
and fell asleep for a hundred years. When she woke up—
What was her name? What? This princess: What was her
name? Oh, I don't know, my child. Some called her Beauty,
I think. That's it, Sleeping Beauty. Have I heard this story
before? Stop interrupting. When she woke up— How did
she wake up? Did a prince kiss her? Ah. No. Well, not then.
There were little babies crawling all over her when she came
to. One of them, searching for her nipple, had found her
finger instead and— Babies? Yes, it seemed that this Sleeping Beauty had been visited by any number of princes over
the years, she was a kind of wayside chapel for royal hunting parties, as you might say, and so there were naturally all
these babies. The one that sucked the thorn out died, of
course, and just as well because in truth she had more of the
demanding little creatures than she and all the fairies who

were helping her could manage. She— Why were they all so little if she'd been asleep a hundred years? Many of them must have grown old and died meanwhile, there must have been old dead bodies lying around. Well, maybe it wasn't exactly a hundred years, Rose, who's to say, maybe it was more like a long winter, what's time to a dreamer, after all? Anyway, when this baby sucked the thorn out, Beauty woke up and found she suddenly had this big family to raise, so when the princes dropped by again for the usual, she made what arrangements were necessary and accommodated them all as best she could, given their modest tastes—I mean, she really didn't have to *do* anything, did she?—and they all became good friends. And everyone lived happily ever after—? Well, they might have if it hadn't have been for the jealous wives. The princes were married—?! Of course, what did you expect, my child? And their wives, needless to say, were fit to be tied. Finally, one day when the princes had all cantered off to war for the summer as princes do, these wives threw a big party at Beauty's place and cooked up all her children in a hundred different dishes, including a kind of hash, sauced with shredded onions, stewed in butter until golden, with wine, salt, pepper, rosemary, and a little mustard added, which they particularly enjoyed. As for

Beauty, that little piece of barnyard offal, as they called her, they decided to slit her throat and boil her in a kind of toad-and-viper soup. Not very nice, but they were so jealous of her they didn't even want her to taste good. Besides, their stomachs were full, the soup would be used to feed the poor. And that's the end of the story? Well, almost. Beauty had been given a lot of pretty presents by her princes, as you can imagine, for they all loved her very much, and they included some lovely gowns in the latest fashion, stitched with gold and silver thread and trimmed with precious jewels, which the wives now fought over, screeching and biting and clawing in the royal manner. They raised such a din that even their princes, far away at war— But it's *terrible!* She would have been better off not waking up at *all!* Well. Yes. I suppose that's true, my dear.

HE ENTERS HER BEDCHAMBER, BRUSHING ASIDE THE THICK dusty webs of a lost century. She lies more upon the bed than in it, propped up in overflowing silks and soft wools and elegant brocades, and delicately aglow in the dusky room as though her unawakened spirit were hovering on her surface like some sort of sorcelous cosmetic. Is she wearing anything? No. Or, rather, yes, a taffeta gown per-haps, deep blue to set off her unbound golden hair, which flows in lustrous rivulets over the feather pillows and bed-ding and over her body, too, as though to illuminate its contours. Her matching slippers are not of leather but also of a heavy blue silk and her stockings, gartered at the knees, are of the purest white. Of course, dark as it is, he might not be able to see all this, though, as he imagines it, dawn is breaking and, as he pushes aside the ancient drapes (he has already, hands now at her knees, pushed them aside, they turned to dust at his touch), the rising sun casts its roseate beams upon her, and especially upon her fair brow, her faintly flushed cheeks, her coral lips, parted slightly to receive his kiss. He pauses to catch his breath, lowers his sword. He has been hacking his way feverishly through the intransigent briar hedge, driven on by his dreams of the prize that awaits him and by his firm sense of voca-tion, but, far from turning to dust at his touch, the hedge has been resisting his every movement, thickening even as he prunes it, snatching at him with its thorns, closing in behind and above him as he advances, if advancing is what he has truly been doing. He should have reached the castle walls long ago. Did he, distracted by the heady blossoms, make a wrong turning, and is he now circling the walls instead of moving toward them? It is impossible to tell, he is utterly enclosed in the briars, could not see the castle turrets even were they still overhead, which, he feels certain (clouds have obscured the moon, all is darkness), they are not. Perhaps, he thinks with a shudder, I have not been chosen after all. Perhaps . . . Perhaps I am not the one.

WELL, EVERYONE *MIGHT* HAVE LIVED HAPPILY EVER AFTER, replies the old crone, gutting a plucked cock, if it hadn't been for his jealous wife. He was married—?! Of course, my love, what did you think? And she was, as you can imagine, a very unhappy lady, even if perhaps she was not the ogress everyone said she was, her husband especially. But that's terrible! That's not the worst of it, I'm afraid. I don't know if I want to hear the rest. She is in the kitchen, which at first was more like her parents' bedchamber or else the bath house, listening to the ancient scold in there tell a story about a princess who fell into an enchanted sleep as a child and woke up a mother. The princess is called Sleeping Beauty, though that might not have been her real name. Has she heard this story before? She can't remember, but it sounds all too familiar, and she is almost certain something bad is about to happen. But she goes on listening because she cannot do otherwise. So she waited until her husband was off hunting or at one of his other houses of pleasure, the old crone continues, ripping out the cock's inner organs, and then she went over to Sleeping Beauty's house and cooked up her children and ordered the clerk of the kitchen to build a big bonfire and burn Beauty alive, calling her a cruel homewrecking bitch and a lump of you-know-what. The kitchen hag, cackling softly, squeezes a handful of chicken guts, making them break wind. There is something vaguely reassuring about this, not unlike a happy ending. The prince's wife, the crone continues, her hands braceleted in pink intestines, had in mind serving up a very special roast to her husband when he got home, believing, you see, that the way to a man's heart is, heh

heh, through the stomach. She sniffs at the cock's tail. The story seems to be over. And that's all? she demands in helpless rage. Not quite, smiles the crone. She shakes her old head and a swarm of blue lights rises and falls around her ears. Sleeping Beauty was wearing a beautiful jewel-studded gown her friend the prince had given her and his wife wanted it, so she ordered Beauty, before being thrown on the fire, to strip down, which she did, slowly, one article at a time, shrieking wildly with each little thing she removed, as though denuding herself was driving her crazy. Meanwhile, as she'd hoped, the prince was just returning from whatever he'd been up to and, on hearing Beauty scream, came running, but before he knew it he found himself in the middle of a huge briar patch. Oh no! Oh yes! He had to cut his way through with his sword, redoubling his effort with each cry of his poor beloved, but the briars seemed to spring up around him even as he chopped them down, and the more she screamed and the more he slashed away, the thicker they got. Yes, yes, I can see him! No, you can't, he was completely swallowed up by the briars. A pity, but it was too late. No! Hurry! Here I am! It's *not* too late!

* * *

Briar Rose

HE IS CAUGHT IN THE BRIARS. THE GNARLED BRANCHES entwine him like a vindictive lover, the thorns lacerate his flesh. Everywhere, like a swampy miasma: the stench of death. He longs now for the solace of the blossoms, their caresses, their fragrance. Ever life's student, he reminds himself that at least he has learned something about the realm of the marvelous, but it does not comfort him. Nothing does, not even fantasies of the beautiful sleeper who lies within, though he does think of her, less now in erotic longing than in sympathetic curiosity. He is young but has adventured the world over, while she, though nearly a century his senior, knows only a tiny corner of a world that no longer even exists, and that but innocently. What kind of a thing is this that jumps about so funnily? she is said to have asked just before being pricked by the fatal spindle and falling into her deep swoon. And now, what if no one ever reaches her, what if she goes on dreaming in there forever, what sort of a life would that be, so strangely timeless and insubstantial? Yet, is it really any different from the life he himself has until now led, driven by his dream of vocation and heroic endeavor and bewitched by desire? Ah, the beautiful: what a deadly illusion! Yet, still he is drawn to it. Still, though all progress through the hedge has been brought to a painful halt and the thorns tear at him with every stroke, he labors on, slashing determinedly at the hedge with his sword, beating back the grasping branches, and musing the while upon this beautiful maiden, fast asleep, called Briar Rose. Does she ever dream of her disenchantment? Does she ever dream of him?

CERTAINLY, SHE DREAMT OF HER SWEETLIPPED PRINCE ALL the time, says the fairy, in reply to Rose's question. But that was not who finally kissed her awake. No? No, in the end she was taken rather rudely by a band of drunken peasants who had broken into the castle, intent on loot. I don't believe this. Of course you believe it, says the fairy. You have no choice. They thought she was dead and commenced to strip her of her finery and naturally one thing led to another and they all had a turn on her, both before she was kissed and after. As the poet put it: Lucky people, so 'tis said,/Are blessed by Fortune whilst in bed. But that's *terrible!* The dreaming child has come to her, fleeing a nightmare about being awakened by an old administrator of her father's kingdom, a stuffy and decrepit ancient with fetid breath, and the fairy has told her an antidotal story about Sleeping Beauty (Have I heard this story before? Rose wanted to know), one of several in the fairy's repertoire, this one with a happy ending. Of course, when the ruffians woke up Beauty they also woke up everything else in the castle, down to the flames in the hearth and the flies on the wall, and including the household knights, who captured the thieves and made them eat their own offending privates before hanging them in the courtyard as an edifying entertainment for the domestic servants, failing to realize that, in effect, they were at the same time severally widowing the poor princess, soon heavy with child. And that was how, fatherless, Dawn and Day were born.

Rose is clearly not consoled by this story. She's had enough, she cries. She wants to wake up. Why me? she demands. Why am I the one? It's not fair!

CAUGHT IN THE BRIARS, BUT STILL SLASHING AWAY VALIANTLY, driven more by fear now than by vocation, he seeks to stay his panic with visions of the sleeping princess awaiting him within, as much in love with her deep repose as with any prospect of her awakening. He has imagined her in all states of dress and undress and in all shapes and complexions, spread out inertly like soft bedding on which to fall and take his ease or springing ferally to life to consume him with her wild pent-up passion, but now he thinks of her principally as a kind friend who might heal his lacerations and calm his anguished heart. It's all right, nothing to fear, dear love, lie back down, it's only a nightmare. Ah, would that it were so! he gasps aloud, his voice sucked up into the dense black night, his desperate heroism's only witness. He pauses to pluck the stinging thorns snagged in his flesh and is immediately pricked by dozens more as the briar hedge, woven tight as a bird's nest, presses up around him. He's not even sure his feet are still on the ground so painfully is he clasped, though he still wears his boots at least, if little else of his princely raiment remains. At times he doubts there is really anyone in the castle, or that there is even a castle, those ghostly turrets glimpsed before notwithstanding. Or if there is a castle and a waiting one within, perhaps it is only the bad fairy who set this task for him and for all these dead suitors, defined their quest with her legendary spite and spindle, this clawing briar hedge the emblem of her savage temper, her gnarled and bitter soul. And even if there is a princess, is she truly the beautiful object of pure love she is alleged to be, or is she, the wicked fairy's wicked creature, more captor than captive, more briar than blossom, such that waking her might have proven a worse fate than the one that is seemingly his, if worse than this can be imagined?

*   *   *

SHE DREAMS OF HER HANDSOME PRINCE, CUTTING HIS WAY through the torturous briars and heroically scaling the high castle walls to reach her bedside and free her from this harsh enchantment. Or perhaps she thinks of him doing so: what, in her suspended condition, is the difference? In either case, there is no residue. Always when she thinks of him, or dreams of him, it is as if for the first time, though she doubts that it can be, there being little else to fill the vast hollow spaces of her pillowed skull but such thoughts, such dreams, and though she remembers very little, she does remember remembering. Moreover, each awakening seems to be enacted against a field of possible awakenings, and how can she know what is possible, even if it is not possible, without, in some manner, remembering it? What she does remember, or believes she does, is being abandoned by her parents on her fifteenth birthday, so little did they care for her and all the omens cast upon her, leaving her once again to her own lonely explorations of the

drafty old castle, explorations which have since provided
the principal settings for all her dreams, or thoughts, but
which on that day led her up a winding staircase to the
secret room at the top of the old tower, there to meet (she
remembers this) her cruel destiny. It's not fair. Why was
she the one? It was nothing bad she had done, she was
famous for her goodness, if anything it was for what she'd
not done, having aroused the wrath of malefic powers,
envious of her goodness and her beauty, or so her ancient
friend in the servery tells her now when she complains, as
she has, as she's told now, so often done. You are one of
the lucky ones, the old crone says, wagging a gnarled finger at her. Your sisters were locked away in iron towers,
lamed and stuck in kitchens, sent to live with savage beasts.
They had their hands and feet cut off, were exiled, raped,
imprisoned, reviled, monstrously deformed, turned to
stone, and killed. Even worse: many of them had their
dreams come true. My sisters? Yes, well, long ago. Dead
now of course.

*   *   *

HER DREAMTIME MORAL LESSONS: OUT ONE EAR AND OUT
the other, as the saying goes. In spite of all the fairy's prom-
ises and reprimands, when the little ninny's not bewailing
her fate, she's doubting it, or if not doubting, dreading it,
afraid of what she longs for. It's frustrating, she simply
cannot, will not learn, and it sometimes makes the fairy,
haunting too long this empty head, lose her temper, even
though she knows that could she, would she, her own
magical ends would surely be thwarted. That the child
sometimes fears what she most desires, the fairy can appreciate, princely heroes being the generally unreliable and
often beastly lot that they are, but that she doubts that her
prince will ever come suggests she underestimates her own
legendary beauty and its power to provoke desire in men.
That such desire is a kind of bewitching (no wonder they
blame it on the fairies!), the fairy knows and uses to her
frequent advantage, though just how it actually works is
something of a mystery to her, one of the main differences

between humankind and fairies being that, for fairies, to desire something is to possess it. The nearest she can come to it is desiring desire itself so as to know the seeming pleasure got from its withheld satisfaction. She is not all-powerful, of course, and so sometimes suffers as well a certain ephemeral longing for the more absolute powers denied her, but, as a caster of spells and a manipulator of plots, the fairy understands that her talents by their very nature assume other powers and prior plots which provide the necessary arena for her transactions; it might even be said that she is empowered by the very powers she lacks, so she cannot really desire them. If, for example, in order to experience desire and its gratification firsthand, she were to try to take Rose's place in the bed and receive her prince (unlike Rose, she *can* learn, *would*), she knows she might lose power over her spell and either reveal herself prematurely or get trapped in her new role with no way to escape it. In a sense, omnipotence is a form of impotence. No, a stool in the servants' quarters of this mooncalf's head where she can sit quietly, filing her teeth, is the closest the fairy can come to witnessing desire's strange mechanisms, or, passing fancies apart, would wish to.

✳   ✳   ✳

ROBERT COOVER

SHE IS AWAKENED BY A BAND OF RUFFIANS, ALL HAVING A GO
on her lifeless body, sometimes more than one at a time.
At first she believes, she doesn't know why, that they are
drunken peasants who have invaded the castle to loot it,
but she soon discovers, recovering somewhat her foggy
wits, that they are her father's household knights. They
seem more dead than alive, ghostly pale, drooling, their
eyes rolled up, showing only the whites. They have roped
her to the bedposts, there is no escape, so she leaves her
struggling there and goes looking for her ancient friend in
the servery, if that's what it is, perhaps it is the great hall,
or even the chapel. Oh mother, she groans, why am I the
one? Because you won't listen! cries the ill-tempered old
scold, flinging the carcass of a plucked goose at her. I'm
sorry, child, she says then, picking up the featherless bird
and sending it flying out the oriel bay window as though
to right a wrong, I didn't mean that, I know you can't help
it, but, believe me, you should stop complaining, you are

one of the lucky ones. And, poking around in her leathery old ear with a blackened claw as though to dig the story out of there (what come out are more of those little blue lights like a swarm of sparkling nits), she tells her about a poor princess married to a wild bear who smelled so bad she had to stuff pebbles up her nose. He pawed her mercilessly and took her violently from behind and bit her when he mated and scratched her with his great horny claws. But the worst thing was his she-bear. He was married—?! Of course, you silly booby, what did you think? The old crone's ferocious tale seems to come alive and she is lying with the stinking bear while his enraged wife snarls and bares her sharp teeth and snaps cruelly at her exposed parts. Why are the crone's stories always about, you know, the natural processes? she asks, though she does not know why she knows this to be so, "always" itself a word whose meaning eludes her. Because, grunts the bear, who seems to be trying to push another painful spindle into her from behind, she's merely an enchantress, my love, it's all the old hag knows.

*   *   *

NOT TRUE; THOUGH, TRUE, IT'S WHAT SHE'S BEST AT, FEEL-
ings and perceptions the very gestures of her intimate art,
the foolish passions of the world-beguiled what best she
can get her iron teeth into. But the prison of the flesh is
not her only theater, the wheel of sensuous agony and
delight not her one and only turn. She is also, in her wag-
gish way, a devotee of the higher learning, an interpreter
and illuminator, concerned with truth and goodness and,
above all, beauty, the mind her stories' true domain, body
merely their comic relief. Though reputed to carry a sack
of black cats on her back and to delight in slitting open
the tums of indolent girls and stuffing them up with scurf
and rubble, she prefers in fact to provision their desolate
heads, ravaged by ignorance and sentiment, and what she
carries on her back, alas, is the weight of eternity, heavy as
a cartload of cowshit. A mere hundred years? It's nothing,
you ninny, she replies to the sniveling dreamer, really you
are one of the lucky ones. And she tells her the story of

the princess chained to a rock thousands of years ago (it seems like only yesterday!) and guarded by a fire-breathing sea monster, who could never understand why this wailing creature, so ruinously chafed by wind and tide, should be thrust upon him like some kind of unanswerable riddle. Well, nothing to do but eat the bony little thing, he supposed, compelled less by appetite than by the mythical proprieties, and he was just tucking dutifully in when a prince turned up intent on rescue, so the dragon asked him in effect the question you have asked. He, too, had no sequential memory, knew only that he was born, so they said, of chaos, she of love, and thus they were cosmological cousins of a sort, and should bear no grudge against one another, so how had they arrived at this moment of mortal encounter, which seemed more theoretical in nature than practical? The prince, well schooled, was interested in this question, touching as it did on the sources of the heroic quest, about which he too sometimes had his misgivings, but the dragon's breath was so hot and noxious all he could do was gasp that it not only always comes down to a family story in the end, but it's always the same one. The monster gaped his jaws in awe of this wisdom and the prince fired a fatal arrow down his throat and into his doubting heart. And they lived happily ever after? How could they, the dragon was dead. No, I mean the princess and the— Oh, who can say? The prince had other tasks and maidens to attend to, making a name for himself as he was, for all I know, my dear, that one's chained there still.

INEXTRICABLY ENSNARED IN THE BRIARS, YET NEVER CEASING to resist (he will remain a hero to the end), he attempts to conjure up an image of the legendary princess who waits inside (but not for him), hoping to assuage his terrible pain and disappointment and stay his rising panic, but it is not her incomparable radiance and beauty that appear to his imagination but more cadaverous traits: her deathly pallor, sunken flesh, crumbling gown, her empty eye sockets. And the ghastly silence that reigns over her. Oh no! Too late! He wets her shrunken bosom with his tears, strokes her cold cheeks, gazes with horror upon her dreadful inertness. He turns her over: her backside is eaten away, crawling with worms and—no, he does not turn her over!

He hacks desperately at the brambles and, as the hedge closes round him like the grasping flesh-raking claws of an old crone, imagines instead her dreams, sweet and hopeful and, above all, loving: loving him who is to come, slashing through the briars and scaling the castle walls to reach her bedside with his spellunbinding kiss. She does not yet dream of that dream-dissolving kiss, however, but rather of his excitement when he discovers her there in all her resplendent innocence, her unconscious body at the mercy of his hungry gaze and impassioned explorations before he quickens it with his kiss, his excitement and her own unwilled passivity before it exciting her in turn, making her eager to awaken and not to awaken at the same time, so delightful is this moment, though of course, he may not be there yet, it is no simple matter to scale the sheer walls of the castle, many have fallen, and once inside he might get lost in the maze of halls and stairs and corridors, not knowing for certain where to find her, and there might be other sleepers along the way who attract his kisses, not to mention his excited explorations, delaying him until it is too late, and even before he can get to the walls there is the infamous briar hedge, noisy with the windblown clatter of bones, the bones of those for whom commitment to love, adventure, honor, and duty and a firm sense of vocation were not enough, their names unmade, forever-aftered into the ignominious anonymity of the nameless dead. No! he cries. Don't just lie there! Get up! Come help!

HER CHARGE HAS JUST EMERGED FROM A NIGHTMARISH awakening in which she was kissed by a toad and turned into one herself and as usual has come running, so to speak, to the fairy, who is calming her with a tale about a beautiful young princess who got pricked one day by a spindle and fell asleep for a hundred years. Have I heard this story before? Hush, child. When she woke up, she found two little babies suckling at her breasts, and one of them— Babies—?! Yes, it seems that her prince, or some prince anyway, had been visiting her person regularly over the years, and these— But didn't the prince kiss her? Didn't he break the spell and wake her up? Well, he may have, I don't know, that's not part of this— But that's *terrible!*

Already she had these babies and she didn't even know if she'd been kissed or not—?! I *hate* this story! All right, wait a minute, let's say he did. He came into the room, greeted the fairies, played with little Dawn and Day, and kissed the princess. That's it? Now what's wrong? It doesn't sound right. It's not like a real story. What do you know about it, you little ninny? snaps the fairy, picking up one of the children and smacking its bottom to, making her point, make it cry: Whose story is this anyway? Rose takes the baby away from her and cuddles it. You really are very wicked, she says, rocking the baby gently in her arms to stop its screaming, and the fairy cackles at that. You're right, she says, when she woke up there weren't any children, that's a different story. Rose stares confusedly into her arms, now cradling empty air. I don't mind, she says timorously, you can leave the babies in if you want. No, no, there were no babies, forget that. Beauty woke up and found not one prince beside her bed, but three: a wizened old graybeard, a leprous hunchback with a beatific smile, and the handsome young hero of her dreams. Which one of you kissed me awake? Beauty asked, looking hopefully at the pretty one. We all did, replied the oldtimer in his creaky voice, and now you must choose between us. Take

the holy one, he said, pointing to the scurvy hunchback
in his haircloth, and your life will be lost to the self-
deceiving confusions of human compassion; take the other
and you must live all your life with lies, deceit, and unre-
strained wickedness. That may be true, old man, said the
beautiful one with a snarling curl of his lip, but at least
I'm not so hard of heart as you. And I live in the real world
of the senses, not some chilly remote tower of the mind.
Look at this! He stripped off his princely finery and, with
a flourish, watching himself in a round gilt-framed mirror
on the wall, struck a pose worthy of the great classic sculp-
tors, with that funny thing between his legs hopping like
a frog. Ah, but remember, said the leper, opening his robes
and, as though in parody, peeling off a wafer of flesh from
his diseased chest, physical beauty is only this deep and
lasts but a brief season, while spiritual beauty lasts forever.
So tell me, my love, says the fairy, scratching her cavern-
ous armpits, which did Sleeping Beauty choose? Oh, I don't
know, whines Rose, and I don't care. You're just making
my head ache. Tell me about the babies again.

*　*　*

HER PRINCE HAS COME AT LAST, HIS CLOTHING SHREDDED from his ordeal in the briars, his stained sword drawn. He slips the blade under her thin gown, grown fragile over the long century of waiting, and with a (her eyes are closed, but she sees all this, knows all this, feels the cold blade slide up her abdomen and between her breasts, watches it lift the gown from her body like a rising tent) quick upward stroke slices it apart. She lies there in all her radiant innocence, exposed to the mercy of his excited gaze, excited by his excitement and by her own feeling of helplessness (she can do nothing about what happens next), and then he kisses her and she awakes. My prince! she sighs. Why have you waited so long? But he has turned away. The room is full of household knights and servants and they are all applauding, her mother and father among them, clapping along with the rest. He sheathes his sword, accepts their cheers and laughter with a graceful bow, blows kisses at the ladies. They gather around him and, chattering gaily, lead him away, fondling his tatters. He does not even look back. Abandoned, she wraps her naked shame in her own hug and drifts tearfully into the nursery or the kitchen, looking for consolation or perhaps some words of wisdom (maybe there are some babies around), but finding instead a door that is not a door. She opens it to the hidden corridor on the other side, which leads, she knows (it's all so familiar, perhaps she wandered here as a child), to a spiral staircase up to a secret tower. Passing the slotted archers' window, she pauses to wonder: is he out there somewhere in the briars? More important: is he really *he?* She climbs the staircase, which winds round and round, up, up, into the shadowy tower above, so high she cannot see from up here where she began below. At the top, behind a creaky old door, she finds a spinning room and an old humpbacked woman in widow's garb, sitting there amid a tangle of unspooled flaxen threads like a spider in her web. Ah, there you are, my pretty, the old crone says, cackling softly. Back for more of the same? Who *am* I? *What* am I? she demands angrily from the doorway, fearing to enter, but fearing even more to back away, uncertain that the stairs she has climbed are still there behind her. It's not fair! Why am I the one?

Briar Rose

HOPELESSLY ENMESHED IN THE FLESH-RENDING EMBRACE OF the briars, he consoles himself with thoughts of what might have been: the legendary princess, his brave overcoming of all obstacles to arrive at her bedside and disenchant her with a magical kiss (he has a talent for it, women have often told him so), her soft expectancy and subsequent adoration of him, his fame and hers and the happiness that must naturally flow therefrom. Around him, the tinkling bones of those nameless brothers he'll soon join speak to him of the vanity of all heroic pursuits and of the dreadful void that the illusions of immortality, so-called, cannot conceal. Well, of course, all life affirmations are grounded in willing self-delusion, masks, artifice, a blind eye cast toward the abyss, this is the very nature of heroism, he knows this, he doesn't need the bones to tell him. Yet still, mad though it may be, he longs to write his name upon the heedless sky. Still (he slashes, a branch falls; it grows back, doubly forked; rearmed, he slashes again), he must strive.

If he were now to reach her bedside and, with his bloody lips, free her from her living death, he would tell her that he did it for love—not for love of her alone, but for love of love, that the world not be emptied of it for want of valor. Would that disappoint her? No, she would understand, she was Beauty, after all, chosen as he was chosen, or as he'd thought he'd been (damn!), and so would know that his kiss, their love, their fated happiness, existed on a plane beyond their everyday regal lives, that theirs has been an emblematic ordeal and a redemption shared with the world. Yes, all right, but it wasn't much of a kiss. What—?! I mean, it was hardly more than a little peck, I didn't even feel it. It was like you really didn't mean it. Oh, he sighs, slashing away bitterly, I guess my mind was elsewhere.

WHEN SHE AWAKENS, HE IS FONDLING HER EXCITEDLY, HIS excitement exciting her (she pleases him!), his touches, too (and he her!), her body tingling with his feverish explorations. It's better even than she imagined it. His delicate

46

hands are everywhere, lightly scrambling up and down her body, it's almost as though he has more than two of them, and he is lashing her with a soft woolly whip, now her thighs, now her face, now her breasts. She smells sweet fennel, balm, lavender, and mint, mixed with dust and less pleasant odors, and she recognizes the smell from her childhood: the rushes strewn with the aromatic herbs on the great hall floor, where she often played beneath the trestle tables while her elders ate. Whom she now hears above her, laughing uproariously. She opens her eyes and sees the monkey perched on her chest between her breasts, smirking at her under the miniature crown tied under his chin. He pinches one pink nipple in his bony little fingers, lifts it and shakes it like a bell, his lips splitting in a maniacal grin, and she feels the ripples all the way to the depths of her belly, where a dull insistent pain resides. Her mother and father and all their friends and all the knights and servants of the castle are gathered around, gazing down with greasy-faced delight upon this spectacle, hooting and laughing and slapping their thighs. They have been eating and drinking, many are eating and drinking still, chewing, spitting, guzzling, and the refuse from their feast is all about her. The monkey rises on all fours, turns his back, lifts his tail to display to her his waxen crimson bottom, and commences to lick and paw between her legs as though picking fleas or searching for something to eat. She feels a burning itch there which she wants desperately to scrub, but she can't move a finger, it's as though all but her intimate parts have been turned to stone. She is terrified and humiliated, but she is also strangely thrilled, not only by the monkey's frolicsome two-handed rummaging, but also by the outrage being committed upon her here, the flaunting of proprieties, the breaking of royal taboos. It's like something is being released, and it feels almost explosive. If only the monkey would stop tickling her and (though she doesn't know what "it" might be) get on with it! That seems to spring a new burst of laughter from her audience, but she is certain she did not speak aloud, cannot. She cannot even cry out as the monkey, losing his temper and snatching and digging at her furiously, slapping, clawing, biting, finally shoving a whole arm inside her, brings back, redoubled, the spindled pain. It's almost as though he wants to break her open, get at what's down deep inside! This is *terrible!* Why are they all laughing?! She's hurting so—! Just then, thankfully, a familiar old crone wanders through, shoos the monkey away (the revelers are gone, vanished, her mother and father among them, as though they never were), melts her petrified limbs, restores her voice to her: Was that it? Has it happened? Has the spell been broken? she gasps, clutching her assaulted parts with both hands. The crone does not reply (they are in the servery now, or maybe the nursery), but instead, cackling softly, says: Calm down, my precious. Let me tell you a story.

ONCE UPON A TIME, THE FAIRY RELATES, THERE WAS A RATHER wild and headstrong little girl who, ignoring the warnings of her elders, climbed up to the top of a secret tower where an old woman was spinning, got pricked by a spindle, and fell asleep for a hundred years. What was her name? I don't know, don't interrupt. It was me, wasn't it? No, Rose, this was someone else. Her name was Beauty, I think. Have I heard this story before? Hush, now! When her hundred years were up, she was awakened by a handsome young prince who loved her very much and visited her whenever he could get away from his wife, which was usually about once every fortnight. He was married——?! Of course he was. Didn't I just tell you? I must have forgotten. But didn't it make her very unhappy——I mean, after waiting all that time——? Yes, it did, but she understood that, being from the last century, she was probably a bit old-fashioned, while he was a modern prince with different ideas, and anyway she had no choice. When the prince's wife, who was an ogress, found out about the affair, she waited until the prince had gone off hunting one day, and then she went over to Beauty's house and ordered the clerk of the kitchen to strip off Beauty's finery, which the wife naturally wanted for herself and without any nasty stains on it, thank you, then to slit her throat and roast her on a spit over the fire. Meanwhile, she prepared a rich garlic soup with spicy fish dumplings, fresh leeks broiled in butter and black pepper, cabbage stuffed with sausage and seasoned with vinegar, mustard, saffron, ginger, and herbs from the garden, fresh baked bread, and for dessert a blancmange flavored with anise. When her husband came back from hunting and saw what she had done, he was very upset of course, Beauty was a special favorite of his, having helped him make his name and all, but he was also very hungry and his wife, who was a wise ogress, had brought along a big jug of delicious young wine from the south to go with the feast she'd prepared, so in the end he settled down and enjoyed his meal, even if he did find the meat a bit tough, being more than a century old as it was. As the ogress had never been able to have any children of her own, she and the prince adopted Beauty's little orphans and took them home with them and they all lived happily ever after. Rose is not amused by this story. It was nothing like that, she complains. What do you know about it, you silly creature? demands the fairy. It is not easy, keeping this going for a hundred years, and she does not appreciate her charge's dismissive attitude. It just doesn't sound right, Rose says. Real stories aren't like that. Real princes aren't.

HER PRINCE HAS COME. THE REAL ONE. IT IS DARK AND SHE does not know where she is but she knows he has come and that it is he. She is filled with rejoicing, but also with trepidation. So much is at stake! She has known all along that her prince would come, but she has also known there

would be no uncoming, forever after as much a threat as
promised delight. What if he is not as she's imagined him
to be? She was safe inside this impenetrable castle, pro-
tected even from the demands of her own body, and now
this alien being who paces at her bedside has broached
those walls and will soon break through to her very core,
if he has not already done so. All her childhood fears re-
turn: of the dark, of strange noises, of monsters and ghosts,
of murderers, of being left alone, of her parents dying, of
getting sick and dying herself, of the world dying. He clears
his throat. Has he kissed her yet? She doesn't remember,
but she musters her courage and opens her eyes to see who
or what is there, terrified now that she will find a great
hairy beast prowling beside her bed. But, no, it is he, a
handsome young prince with manly brow and beard and
flowing locks, tall and lean and strong. My prince, she
whispers. You have come at last! Yes, well, he says with
a grimace, wandering distractedly through the dimly lit
room, draped in swags of gray dusty webs, which he swipes
at irritably with his gauntleted hand. At a wooden chest,
he picks up a bonehandled copper pitcher enameled with
the family crest, thumps it, peers at its green bottom, sets
it down again. He pokes through some wardrobe draw-

ers, raising clouds of dust, finds some rings and necklaces
and silver pennies, which he sorts through idly. Perhaps
he takes some of these things, but not as a thief might: in
effect, he *possesses* them. With one metallic finger he strokes
a plump lute resting on a table: the dry strings snap and
ping, their ancient tension released, but not hers. My
prince? He turns his restless gaze upon her for a moment
and then it seems to pierce right through her, as though
focusing on something within or beyond her, chilling her
to the marrow before it drifts away again, coming to rest
on a chessboard with cracked and yellowed ivory pieces.
He moves one of the figures, freeing it from its bonds of
web, then, with a shrug, tips it over. It is a delicate, casual,
yet studied gesture, and it terrifies her. In front of a round
dust-grimed mirror on the wall, he stares at himself, strok-
ing his beard. He is immaculately groomed and dressed,
more elegant even than she had dreamt he would be. You
are very beautiful, she murmurs timidly, but I thought you'd,
I don't know, show more outward signs of your terrible
ordeal. Ordeal—? You know, the briars. He turns away from
the mirror, peers at her warily with narrowed eyes. What
briars? Didn't you have to cut your way through a briar hedge
outside? Maybe, he says stonily, I'm at the wrong castle.

HE HAS, IN HIS IMAGINATION (ALL THAT'S LEFT HIM), SLASHED his way through the briars, scaled the castle wall, and reached her bedside. He had expected to be aroused by the mere sight of her, this legendary beauty both doelike and feral, and indeed, stripped naked by the briars, his flesh stinging still from the pricking of the thorns which he seems to be wound in now like a martyr's shroud, he is aroused, but not by the grave creature who lies there before him, pale and motionless, wearing her ghostly beauty like an ancient ineradicable sorrow. His sense of vocation propels him forward and, pushed on by love and honor to complete this fabled adventure, he leans forward to kiss those soft coral lips, slightly parted, which have waited for him all these hundred years, that he might unbind her from her spell and so fulfil his own emblematic destiny. But he hesitates. What holds him back? Not this hollow rattle of old bones all about. Something more like compassion perhaps. What is happily ever after, after all, but a fall into the ordinary, into human weakness, gathering despair, a fall into death? His fate to be sure, whether he makes his name or not (what does it matter?), but it need not be hers. He imagines the delirium of their union, the celebrations and consequent flowering of the moribund kingdom, the offspring that would follow, the joys thereof, the pains, the Kingship, the Queenship, her obligations, his, the days following upon days, the exhaustion of the "inexhaustible fountain of their passion," the disappointments and frustrations and betrayals, the tedium, the doubts (was it really she after all? was it really he?), the disfigurements of time, the draining away of meaning and memory, the ensuing silences, the death of dreams; and, enrobed in pain, willfully nameless, yet in his own way striving still, he slips back into the briars' embrace.

THE FAIRY SITS SPINNING IN THE TOWER, ENTANGLED IN HER storied strands, joining thread to thread, winding them into seductive skeins, awaiting the dreamer's visit, her accusations, her demands. It has not been easy, trying to fill her limboed head through all this time, by some calendars as much as a century or more, so from time to time over the years (call them that), in order to rehearse her craft, respell the wound, she has returned here to the source. The scene, as they say, of the crime. Of course, given the child's inability to put any two thoughts together in succession or to hold either of them between her ears longer than it takes to think them, the fairy might just as well tell the same story over and over again, and indeed she has repeated most of them, one time or another, it has been a long night. But, for her own sake more than her auditor's, fearing to lose the thread and sink away herself into a sleep as deep as that she inhabits, thus gravely endangering them both, she has sought, even while holding fast to her main plot, to tell each variant as though it had never been told before, surprising even herself at times with her novelties. She has imagined, and for Rose described, a rich assortment of beauties and princes, obstacles, awakenings, and what-happened-nexts, weaving in a diverse collection of monsters, dragons, ogres, jests, rapes, riddles, murders, magic, maimings, dead bodies, and babies, just to watch the insatiable sleeper wince and gasp and twitch with fear and

longing, wicked fairy that she is. She has rarely gone afield
in her tales, wandering instead the tranced castle, using it
some times as a theatrical contrivance, others as a kind of
house of the dead, touring intimately its most secret re-
cesses. Castle-bound as the dreamer is, the illusion of
boundaries, above all that of the body, has been one of
the fairy's frequent themes, along with the contest between
light and dark, the passions of jealousy and desire, canni-
balism, seduction and adultery, and the vicissitudes of day-
to-day life in the eternal city of the tale, the paradoxes
thereof. That between gesture and language, for example.
This she illustrated one day, when asked, But why does
he have to *kiss* her, by describing in exhaustive detail every
nuance of the sleeper's expression as witnessed by the
hovering prince, down to the subtle chiaroscuro of light
as it grazed her brow at different angles and the movement
of the fine hairs in her nostrils, a cartographical epic that
might have gone on without lips meeting lips for the rest
of the century, had not her capricious audience, screaming for release, retreated in spite to a passing nightmare
about a prince who awoke her by sinking his teeth suddenly into her throat.

✳   ✳   ✳

THOUGH HE NO LONGER EVEN WISHES TO REACH HER, TO wake her, he continues, compelled by vocation, to slash away at his relentless adversary, whose deceptive flowers have given the object of this quest the only name he knows. Though she remains his true love, salvation and goal, the maker of his name, jewel at the core, and all that, he cannot help but resent her just a little for getting him into this mess, which is probably fatal. She is beautiful, true, perhaps the most beautiful creature in the world, or so they say, and, in his agony, he has consoled himself with thoughts about her, principally of an amorous nature, it being that sort of adventure, but he has also thought often about his life before he undertook this quest, its simple sensible joys, the freedom of it, the power he wielded, the fame and honor he enjoyed, even if all much less than her disenchantment might have provided, had he been the one chosen for it. He has imagined, having first imagined the eventual success of this enterprise, explaining to her, or trying to explain, his con-

tinuing attraction to that former life in order to suggest a
distinction between his breaking of her spell and the happily-
ever-after part, the latter to be negotiated separately, and,
so doing, has grasped something of the true meaning of her
name, for clearly, from her perspective, this hundred years'
wait has not prepared her to tolerate such a distinction. In
short, at the least hint of his choosing other than the either
of her either/or, she has seemed prepared (in his imagination) to scratch his eyes out. Which in turn has offered him
an insight into a possible way out of here: could it be that,
in struggling against the briars, he might in fact be struggling only against something in himself, and that therefore,
if he could come to understand and accept the real terms of
this quest, the briars might simply fade away? Or is that what
all these other clattering heroes thought?

SHE HAS TOLD HER (THE LITTLE DIMWIT HAS FORGOTTEN
this, perhaps she will tell it again) about the prince who,
trapped in the briars, was given three wishes and wasted

them by first wishing himself in Beauty's bedroom, which he found empty, then wishing to know where she was, and, on learning she was in the very hedge he'd been trapped in, wishing himself back in the briars again, though the wishes weren't completely wasted because at least now, on a clear day when their shouts carried, he had company in his suffering. The fairy recognizes that many of her stories, even when by her lights comic, have to do with suffering, often intolerable and unassuaged suffering, probably because she truly is a wicked fairy, but also because she is at heart (or would be if she had one) a practical old thing who wants to prepare her moony charge for more than a quick kiss and a wedding party, which means she is also a good fairy, such distinctions being somewhat blurred in the world she comes from. Thus, her tales have touched on infanticide and child abuse, abandonment, mutilation, mass murder and cruel executions, and, in spite of the subjects, not all endings have been happy. She has told her the story of the musicians at Beauty's wedding feast who distracted the bride with their flutes and tambourines and kettledrums, while their dancing girls were off seducing the groom, thereby sending him to his nuptial bed with a dreadful social disease. She has told her (also forgotten) of a monstrously evil Sleeping Beauty and of the horrors unleashed upon the prince and all the kingdom when he awakened her, as well as of the hero under a beastly spell who ate Beauty immediately upon finding her so as to avoid returning to his dreary life as a workaday prince, adding a few diverting notes about his digestive processes just to stretch the tale out. But stories aren't like that, the ill-tempered child will inevitably insist, and the fairy only cackles sourly at that and tells another. She will be up here soon. Now she's found the way, she cannot help but keep coming back. But it always takes her a while to find it. Rose imagines this ancient spinning room in the tower to be an impossible distance away, through hidden corridors and up rickety stairwells, not realizing that it is, so to speak, just behind her left ear . . .

WHEN HE FINALLY, WITH A LAST DESPERATE STROKE, SLASHED through and emerged from the dark night of the briars, he found that day had broken and the world had changed.

He'd evidently lost his way inside the hedge and got turned around, for there was his horse, still tethered where he'd left him. But the forest he'd tethered him in was gone. Everything was gone. As far as he could see: a vast barren landscape under the noonday sun. A fairy came, the horse explained, and took everything away. What—? The horse could talk—? Of course it could talk, says the old crone irritably, peering up at her from her spinning wheel. What's wrong with that? I don't know, it just doesn't seem right. She wonders if her own prince could have a talking horse, and since, in her stuporous condition, thinking and speaking are the same thing, the crone replies: A talking horse? Don't be ridiculous! Why do you always suppose every story is about you? Now come on in here and stop interrupting. She remains in the drafty doorway, afraid to enter (something bad has happened here) but afraid to back away, uncertain if the spiral staircase she has climbed is still there behind her. She does not like this story, but knows that its teller knows this without her having to say so. Little blue sparks fly as the crone, turning the wheel slowly, lets the flax slide through her old gnarled fingers. The prince, she continues, wanted to know what the fairy looked like, what color was she, how many teats did she have, was she good or bad, did she come from outside or inside? Inside what? asked the horse. The hedge, stupid, said the prince with an impatient gesture. But then he saw that the hedge was gone, too, they were all alone in the blazing emptiness. He thought about this for a moment, and then he said: Maybe everything is really still here. Maybe it only appears to our bewitched senses to be gone. That may seem reasonable to you, snorted his horse, but it doesn't make my kind of sense. No, really, insisted the prince, it's one of the fairies' favorite tricks. So maybe now, knowing this, I can finally get through to the hidden castle and break the spell. Is this possible? Can he do it? Her interest in the story has picked up, and she takes a tentative halfstep into the room, bringing a curling smile to the dry lips of the old crone. So the prince raised his sword and, bracing himself for the worst, went charging about under the hot sun like one possessed, hoping to bump up against something solid, but in the end all he got out of it was sunblindness and a terrible thirst. The horse snickered at all this human folly and said they should move on and try to find something to eat, but the prince, who was on a heroic quest which he felt determined to see through to the end, even if seeing was no longer what he did best, stubbornly refused, so the horse trotted off without him. The prince went on frantically hunting for the invisible castle for the rest of his life, which was not long, there being nothing to eat in that desert but sand. He died——? Oh yes, raisined up like a dogturd out there in the sun, my pet, a worshipful sight. They would have made him a saint, but they didn't know what to call him since he had failed in his quest and so had never made his—— No, she insists from the doorway, backing away. You can't do that. That's not how stories are.

THE MORE THE POSSIBILITY OF REACHING HER BEDSIDE recedes, the closer he seems to come to her. He does not know if, consumed by fear and desire, he is generating this illusion himself, or if it is fairy magic. But he is scaling the castle walls before he has escaped the briars, exploring the castle before he has scaled the walls. It feels as if an impossible problem is being solved, all by itself. The castle itself is a strange and haunted place, unlike any he has ever

seen before, yet also oddly comforting, more like home
than home. Searching for her through its webby mazes,
he feels like he is opening doors to his own past, though
it is more like a past that might have been than a real one.
Before he has found her, he is already at her bedside. He
is so stunned by her beauty, he can't move, even though
his lips are already approaching hers. He thinks: Won't it
all be spoiled if I wake her up? But he has already awakened her: they are in the great hall, or else in front of the
oriel window, gazing out on the manicured gardens, bor-
dered by a small trimmed hedge of sweetbriar. She is just
as he has imagined her: beautiful, gentle, innocent, devoted,
submissive. He is suffused with love and desire, but he also
feels like he would like to take a nap. Today, she says, I
saw a strange thing. I saw a plucked goose flying. It flopped
into my room where I was sleeping or else lying awake and
said to me: You will never awaken because the story you
were in no longer exists. Oh yes? He is thinking about the
quest that brought him here. Has he made his name then?
If so, what is it? Or has he perhaps come to the wrong castle?
When she says, perhaps not for the first time, that, even when
sitting in the same room with him, she feels like she's all
alone, he realizes his mind has been elsewhere. I'm sorry,

my love, he says. What is your heart's desire? To live happily ever after, she replies without emotion. Of course, he replies, it's yours for the asking. And also I wonder if you'd mind watching the babies for a while? Babies—?!

SHE IS IN THE KITCHEN, OR ELSE THE NURSERY, PLAYING with the babies. They seem to have been conjured up by one of the old crone's tales, but she's glad they're there, strange as they are, more like her parents than any children, the boy with his little tuft of beard, the girl gazing upon her in haughty disapproval even as she changes her breechcloth. The crone, stirring a thick steamy brew in a cauldron big as a bathtub, hung over the fire on an iron chain (they *are* in the kitchen then, or else in the bedchamber and that *is* a bathtub), is telling her a story about a princess guarded by a fire-breathing dragon known for his ferocity and his insatiable appetite for tender young maidens, breath-roasted while spitted on a claw. The crone provides several of the dragon's favorite recipes for basting and dipping sauces, which Rose does not find amusing. Usually—if one with a memory such as hers can really have any idea about what might be usual—she is alone in the castle with the old crone, but sometimes it is full of other people, servants, knights, even princes, and the children come and go at random (they are gone now), an arrangement which also somewhat perplexes her, though only when she imagines she is awake, not often. Today she was fooled by a prince who approached her bedside and began probing her as though examining her systematically for the source of her spindled pain. He was tall and handsome, but badly wounded, his clothing shredded and clinging to him by bloody tatters. My prince! You have come at last! Yes, well, it was a matter of honor, he said gravely, disappointing her. I did it for the love of love. But what kind of a thing is that that jumps about so funnily? she added sleepily, although it was not what she had meant to say at all, it just seemed to pop to mind. For providing relief from sorrow and contact with the numinous, he replied tersely, even as his fingers burrowed deeper. Though it is all an illusion of course. Yes, I know, she sighed and opened her eyes. No prince. Of course. Just a family of nesting churchmice, scurrying beneath her gown. She closed her eyes again and, without transition, found herself here in the kitchen, where now the old crone is down on her haunches, adding a few sticks of firewood to the embers and fanning them into flames with her thick layers of smelly black skirts. In her story, the hero has just flown in with the head of a lady with snaky hair that turns everyone into statues. He aims the frightful thing at the dragon, but the dragon ducks and looks away and the head stuns the princess instead. Now she's useless to everyone. She may have heard this story before, the part about a princess turned to stone is familiar, but she can't be sure. What was the princess's name? she asks. Don't interrupt! snaps the old crone, shaking the slotted spoon at her, sparks flying from her clashing teeth, her wild unkempt hair twisting about her head like a nest of vipers. She ladles something out of the cauldron that looks like another baby. The important question, you little ninny (her own knees and elbows have gone numb, perhaps she has been lying too long in the same position), is whose head was he using?

✳   ✳   ✳

Briar Rose

SEARCHING IN HIMSELF FOR THE MAGICAL KNOWLEDGE THAT might make the murderous briars sheathe their thorns and fade away, he has seemed to hear the sleeping princess say (perhaps this is just before awakening her, or perhaps it is years later): There is a door that is not a door. That is where it all begins. He knows that nothing at this castle is simply what it is, everything here has a double life, so he supposes she is trying to tell him something else, the way out of this thorny maze, for example, or the way in to her own affections. She is in front of a mirror (the doubled re-doubled), letting down her golden hair. Her beauty numbs him. Now that I am awake, she says, the truth is more hidden than before. Her mirrored eyes meet his: When will this spell be broken? she asks. When will my true prince come? So, as he feared: he is not the one. Or perhaps he is the one, or could be, this her plea that he become the prince she has been dreaming of. He does indeed feel himself becoming that imagined prince, and he wonders if perhaps she is a sorceress. His doubts darken her countenance, either with sorrow or with anger. Or with desire. She holds the mirror up to his face and he sees something hairy and toothy, halfway between a wolf and a bear, and he feels overwhelmed by lust and stupidity, a not unpleasant sensation, the best he's had probably since he set forth upon this adventure. It doesn't last, forget happily ever after, she is dressing him in pretty new clothes with all the needles left inside and leading him by the paw into the great hall for the castle ball. As he enters the hall, engulfed in pain, he realizes he has arrived at the perilous edge of the world and that from this entering there will be no departing. Help! he howls. Wake up! Get me out of here!

SHE IMAGINES HIM (A CONJURING OF SORTS) SOMEHOW SCAL-ing the unscalable walls and, his flesh stinging still from the barbed briars, searching through the webbed labyrinth of the ancient castle for the bedchamber of the legendary sleeping princess, but finding instead a door that is not a door, leading down a secret corridor to a spiral staircase. He climbs it, sword drawn, and, in a room at the top of the tower, finds a beautiful maiden with flaxen hair spinning alone by candlelight. Ah, there you are! she exclaims breathlessly. You have come at last! That's strange, I was told you would be sleeping, he says. I couldn't wait, she replies with a seductive smile. Now come on in here and close the door, you're letting in a draft. He hesitates, framed by an abysmal darkness, his sword still drawn, then looks away, keeping her only in the corner of his eye, no doubt hoping to catch her changing back to her real shape when she thinks she is not being watched. Ah, nothing worse, from the fairy's point of view, than a cogitative prince. Brave and handsome, yes, and perhaps a few of the social graces, a smooth dancer, comfortable with the clichés: Charming, as they're so often called. But not too much introspection, thank you, not too much heavy pondering, else the game's up for distressed maidens like her present seeming self, who weeps now as though her heart has been broken. You don't love me! she sobs. You are not the one! Yes, I am! he cries, sheathing his sword and rushing to her side. I'm sorry, my love! He falls to one knee and clasps her to his wounded bosom. That's better. But it's so hard to know what's real and not in such a place, he pleads. I know, I know, she groans, hugging him tight, pressing the thorns in deeper. She has one hand between his legs, peeling away the bloody tatters that remain. I'm such a silly goose, she sighs, smiling tenderly at him, her iron teeth, she knows, glinting like nuggets of gold in the guttering candlelight, a voluptuous sight not even she, in his boots, could resist. Then, with a rueful sigh (such is the fairy's lonely burden!), she unravels the knots, loosing thread from thread, and, allowing her hump to rise once more, her hide to hornify, her multitude of breasts to fall, commences to spin again. Desire: what is it exactly?

SHE IS SEATED BESIDE THE KING AT THE HIGH TABLE IN THE great hall. He looks like her father, yet is not her father. There is something heavy weighing on her head which makes her want to lie down under the table and go to sleep. She touches it: a crown. A great span of time seems to have passed since her awakening, which she cannot at the moment remember. Or, more likely, she is still asleep and dreaming, this merely another of the old crone's wicked entertainments. The room is full of banqueters and servants but they are not moving or speaking. Perhaps they have been turned to stone. Two naked children, who may be hers, are playing in the dirty rushes under the trestle tables, their rosy bottoms bobbing like apples in a tub of dirty water, the only things moving in the hall. She would like to give them both a good spanking, or else go play with them (she could be the dragon), but she is too tired to move. Happily ever after, the king says. It's never quite like you imagine it. She nods. A mistake. The weight of her crown carries her head all the way into her plate of food. She has, literally, to lift her head with both hands and put it upright on her shoulders again. Time disfigures everything, he sighs and belches, scratching his hairy belly. But at least we have our memories. We do? An ancient humpbacked creature shuffles in from the kitchen and gives her a cloth with which to wipe the gravy from her face. One of the old crone's petticoats, by the smell of it. Of course we do. Don't you remember the musical parade at our wedding feast, this crowned and bearded stranger asks, the flutes and trumpets, the kettledrums, the tambourines? No . . . The dancing girls? She flies into a sudden rage and wheels round to dig her nails into his face, her crown toppling. She claws deep red grooves through his cheeks. He does not resist. You are not the one! she screams. His beard, catching the rivulets of blood, seems to whiten as though a century were passing. Sometimes, he says, gazing at her tenderly as if indeed he might know her or have known her once upon a time, I feel the reason I never escaped the briars was that, in the end, I loved them, or at least I needed them. Let's say, he adds with a curling smile, licking at the blood at the corners of his lips, they grew on me . . .

ALTHOUGH STILL TRAPPED IN THE HEDGE, HE HAS SOMEHOW clawed his way through, scaled the castle walls, awakened the sleeping princess, broken the spell, and saved the moribund kingdom. Even the flies, they say, got up off the wall and flew again. But it all happened so long ago, his memory of it is as though a borrowed one, and he feels substantially unrewarded for all his pain and suffering. Which she, for one (the entire kingdom is another), has never truly appreciated, taking it all for granted as part of the devotion due her. Or else doubting it altogether, as she doubts him: Are you really the one? she will ask from time to time, gazing darkly at him with fear and suspicion. Perhaps not, he thinks, licking his unhealed wounds. Perhaps I have come to the wrong castle. When he first arrived here, or imagined arriving here, it was like returning home again, so familiar was it. He knew, for example, even before escaping the briars, just where the sleeping princess lay. But it may be that his knowing was itself part of the spell, for the castle has grown in strangeness ever since. Or perhaps he has grown more complex, his quest less clear and pure, the castle recognizable only to an unmazed mind. He can no longer even find at will her sleeping chamber, though he is often in it, transported there as though by sorcery when simplified by desire and wine, or by his terror of the briared night. What happens there is a periodic reminder to him of the brevity of all amorous pursuits and the symmetries of love and death, and seems intended to recall for him, or perhaps for her, that night he is said to have first

awakened her: the stale morbidity of the bed in which she
lay, canopied in dark dusky webs, its linens eaten by the
vermin scurrying within, she spread upon it like a sentient
bolster, so sweetly vulnerable, hands crossed primly on her
pubescent breast, knees together, the rouge of her cheeks
and the coral of her parted lips like painterly touches of
the embalmer's art, her gown a silky gauze turned by time
to dust that vanished in a puff when he blew upon it, or
so she has told him, explaining the powdering of her body
and what he must do now to please her. These nightly
rituals pass like dreams, or rather like a single dream
redreamt, so indistinguishable are they from one another,
which also seems a portion of her pleasure. Yes, yes, that's
how it was! Her obsessive recreations of love's awakening
delirium are perhaps what most oppress him, not because,
as he blows the dust away, they cast a shadow of what
might have been upon their workaday royal lives, but because they suggest to him what might yet, if he could but
escape this castle, be. He hears rumors of enchanted prin-
cesses out on the perilous fringe, asleep for a hundred years
or more, and longs to ride out once again on new adventure, to tame mystery and make his name in the old way,
but she does not understand such restlessness, she was born

to these stacked stones, so haunted by her dreams, it's all
the life she knows or wants to know, heroic endeavor a
kind of wickedness to her, all quests but one unholy. When
he makes the mistake of announcing to all present at high
table in the great hall his noble intention to sally forth to
rescue another sleeping maiden, she explodes with sudden
fury, clawing at his face as though to scratch his eyes out,
and then, just as suddenly, falls asleep with her face in the
soup, provoking a general alarm. The chamberlain hauls
her out of the soup by her golden hair and the sauce cook
throws water on her, her lady-in-waiting unlaces her cor-
sets and rubs her temples with eau de cologne, the chap-
lain slaps her hands and the kitchen boy her face, but
nothing wakes her. He can feel their hostility mounting,
the hairs bristling on his snout and back. His wounded
face burns with pain and chagrin. I'll never get out of here,
he laments. The others circle round, their faces going slack,
eyes narrowing to dark bloody slits. All right, all right, he
barks irritably, lifting her up and carrying her out of the
great hall toward her bedchamber. I'll do it!

※　　※　　※

SHE AWAKENS TO REPEATED AWAKENINGS AS THOUGH trapped in some strange mechanism, and she longs now to bring it to a standstill, to put an end once and for all to all disquiet, even if it means to sleep again and sleep a dreamless sleep. And so she goes in search of an old crone who has befriended her, one she believes may have magical powers, or at least some useful pharmaceutical ones, and while looking for her she comes upon a door that is not a door. She knows, though she does not know how she knows, that beyond it there is a long dark corridor leading to a spiral staircase, at the top of which, in the highest tower of the castle, is a spinning room. Where something bad happened. Or will happen. But something perhaps that she desires. She steps through into the secret corridor and there discovers her true prince in all his manly radiance embracing a scullery maid. Oh, sorry, he says. But she was asleep and I was only trying to— She wants to scratch his eyes out, but he has already disappeared. She seems to hear galloping hooves, though it may be only the clattering of her unhappy heart. Perhaps he has abandoned her forever, returning to his ogress wife or riding off to new adventures. It is easy for him. She has no horse, could not steer it if she did, would not know where to take it if she could, this castle all she knows or dares to know. Such a ninny, as the old crone says. But his exuberance frightens her, his worldly heroics do. He is young enough to be her great-great-great grandson, yet he seems a hundred years older. Sometimes I think it was better when we was all asleep, mum, the maid says wistfully, hands cupped under her belly, swollen with child. I had such pretty dreams then. Yes, I know. She will have the girl's throat slit tomorrow and serve her up to him when he returns, his unborn between her jaws like a baked apple, if tomorrow ever comes, but for now, feeling like an abandoned child, those who might protect her from the fairy's curse gone off to their houses of duty or pleasure, she continues her lonely explorations, down the shadowy corridor and up the swaying spiral staircase, her eyes closed, hands crossed demurely on her breast, her silken gown disintegrating in the chill draft, lips parted slightly to receive what fate awaits her.

THE BAD FAIRY, WHO IS ALSO THE GOOD FAIRY, RETURNING to the source as she so often does, finds her unhappy charge sprawled on the floor of the spinning room, clothed in little more than tangled flaxen strands and furiously stabbing herself over and over with the spindle. Ah, such a desire to sleep again, the fairy muses, reckoning the poor creature's tormented thoughts. She could well change herself into a handsome prince and give her a consolatory kiss and a cuddle, but, in the state she is in, it might only provoke her into throwing her disembodied self down the stairwell, augmenting her confusion and despair. Will this spell never be broken? Rose wants to know. The warring sides of the fairy's own nature clamor for attention: isn't it time to dip into your necromantic bag of tricks for a little relief, you old bawd, a bit of allegorical hocus-pocus perhaps, that old scam? The good fairy's boon to this child, newborn, was to arrange for her to expire before suffering the misery of the ever-after part of the human span, the wicked fairy in her, for the sake of her own entertainment, transforming that well-meant gift to death in life and life in death without surcease. And, in truth, she *has* been entertained, is entertained still. How else pass these tedious centuries? Once upon a time, she says with a curling smile, her wicked side as usual taking over, there was a handsome prince and a beautiful princess who lived happily ever after. But that's *terrible!* cries Rose. No, no, wait, that's just the beginning. But I *hate* this story! Happily ever after, admonishes the fairy, wagging a gnarled finger the color of pig iron. It may not be worth a parched fig, my daughter, but it hides the warts, so don't be too quick to throw it out! You really are evil, Rose groans, continuing to stab herself without mercy. Yes, well, what did you expect, you little ninny? But put that spindle down. Haven't I told you a thousand times——? She ignores her, hammering away at the center of her pain like some strange mechanism gone amok, so the fairy turns the spindle into a slimy green frog that squirts out of her hand and, croaking frantically like one escaping a thorny entrapment, hops away, leaving Rose weeping pathetically, now utterly forlorn. All right then, my love. Listen up. Once upon a time . . .

*   *   *

FROM HIS DAIS CHAIR AT THE HIGH TABLE HE HAS ANNOUNCED to everyone in the great hall that he has heard of another enchanted princess, some leagues distant, who has slept for a hundred years, and that he now intends to ride out to find her and, if possible, to break the ancient spell. As a royal prince, dedicated to virtuous exploits of this nature, it is the least he can do, for the sake of the stricken kingdom as much as for the maiden. So, pushed on by love and honor, he has kissed his wife good-bye (or would have, had she let him) and sallied forth to confront evil, tame mystery, make his name. At the castle gates, he encounters an old webfooted hunchback who gives him a boon and a prophetic warning. Her boon is a magic ointment that will drive off wicked sorceresses and also restore hair, heal unnatural wounds, and revive manly vigor. The warning is: Take along the old weird's head, when you approach the enchanted bed. And she seems to take off her own and offer it to him. He laughs, confident of his own princely powers, and the crone, cackling along with him, disappears as though suddenly turned to dust. He journeys for many years, following the conflicting advice of countrymen met on the way, until he arrives at an enchanted forest near the edge of the world and is directed to a dark gloomy castle, said to be haunted by spirits and ogres and to contain in its depths a sleeping princess who has lain there as though dead for a hundred years. Yes, I know, that is why I am here, he says. It is my vocation. Over the years, brambles have grown up around the castle, leaving only the pale moonlit turrets and battlements visible. It will not be easy, but this, too, he has anticipated, for the pursuit of a noble quest, he knows, is ever arduous and fraught with peril. He tethers his steed, draws his sword, and steps boldly into the dense overgrowth without looking back. Fortunately, he has arrived when the thicket is in full bloom. He has left the crone's ointment back in his saddlebag, but he won't need it, even were it what the old fraud claimed it to be: the branches part gently, the fragrant petals caress his cheeks. He is surprised how easy it is. How familiar. He feels, oddly, like he's coming home again. It is not the castle, no, nor the princess inside (perhaps he will reach her and disenchant her with a kiss, perhaps he will not; it matters less than he'd supposed), but this flowering briar patch, hung with old bones, wherein he strives. I am he who awakens Beauty, the bones seem to whisper as the blossoms enfold him.

SHE LIES ALONE IN HER DUSKY BEDCHAMBER ATOP THE morbid bed. Perhaps she has never left it, her body anchored forever here by the pain of the spindle prick, while her disembodied self, from time to time, goes aimlessly astray, drifting through the castle of her childhood, in search of nothing whatsoever, except perhaps distraction from her lonely fears (of the dark, of abandonment, of not knowing who she is, of the death of the world), which gnaw at her ceaselessly like the scurrying rodents beneath her silken chemise. If she is still asleep, it does not feel like sleep, more like its opposite, an interminable wakefulness from which she cannot ease herself, yet one that leaves no residue save echoes of an old crone's tales, and the feeling that her life is not, has not been a life at all. Sometimes, in her wanderings, she finds a castle populous with sleepers, frozen in their tracks, snoring pimply-faced guards clutching wineglasses in which the dregs have dried, round-bellied scullery maids sweeping, their stilled labor swagged in thick dusty webs, the cook with a fistful of the kitchen boy's hair, his cuffing stopped in sudden sleep. But if she opens her eyes again, the castle will be dark and empty, hollow with a chill wind blowing, or else suddenly filled with a bustling confusion of servants, knights, children, animals, husbands or lovers, all making demands upon her, demands she cannot possibly fulfill, or even understand, and all she longs for, as she tells the old crone in the tower, is to sleep again. The crone may cackle or tell a story or scold her for her self-absorption, but sooner or later she will open her eyes and find herself here in her moldy bed once more, waiting for she knows not what in the name of waiting for her prince to come. Of whom, no lack, though none true so far of course, unless in some strange wise they all are, her sequential disenchantments then the very essence of her being, the fairy's spell binding her not to a suspenseful waiting for what might yet be, but to the eternal reenactment of what, other than, she can never be. She closes her eyes to such a cruel fate, but, as always, it is as if she has opened them again, and now to yet another prince arriving, bloodied but exultant, at her bedside. She welcomes him, cannot do other, ready as always for come what may. He leans toward her, blows her dessicated gown away. Yes, yes, that's right, my prince! And now, tenderly if you can, toothily if need be, take this spindled pain away . . .